Rabbi Nosson Scherman / Rabbi Meir Zlotowitz
General Editors

CHAVIVA KROHN PFEIFFER
Maggid Stories
Illustrated by
Chani Stern
Published by
Mesorah Publications, ltd

for Children
Holidays
and
Around the Year

MAGGID STORIES FOR CHILDREN — HOLIDAYS AND AROUND THE YEAR

First edition – First impression: March, 2008

Published by **MESORAH PUBLICATIONS, LTD.**
4401 Second Avenue / Brooklyn, N.Y 11232 / (718) 921-9000 / Fax: (718) 680-1875
www.artscroll.com

Distributed in Israel by SIFRIATI / A. GITLER
6 Hayarkon Street / Bnei Brak 51127

Distributed in Europe by J. LEHMANN HEBREW BOOKSELLERS
Unit E, Viking Industrial Park, Rolling Mill Road / Jarrow, Tyne and Wear / England NE32 3DP

Distributed in Australia and New Zealand by GOLD'S BOOK & GIFT SHOP
3-13 William Street / Balaclava, Melbourne 3183, Victoria, Australia

Distributed in South Africa by KOLLEL BOOKSHOP
Ivy Common / 105 William Road / Norwood 2192, Johannesburg, South Africa

Printed in the United States of America by Noble Book Press Corp.
Bound by Sefercraft, Quality Bookbinders, Ltd., Brooklyn, N.Y. 11232

ISBN 10: 1-4226-0648-1 / ISBN 13: 978-1-4226-0648-3

Table of Contents

Author's Preface

I am grateful to the *Ribono Shel Olam* for having given me the opportunity to write a third book of stories, culled from the Maggid books written by my father, Rabbi Paysach Krohn. It is hoped that these stories will inspire young readers to improve in their *zehirus b'mitzvos* and *middos tovos*.

The *Yamim Tovim* elicit specific emotions in our hearts and homes. The warmth of Chanukah, the solemnity of Yom Kippur, the festivity of Purim, and the royalty of Pesach cannot be captured with such intensity at any other time of the year. Many of our childhood memories revolve around these special days.

Anticipation for each Yom Tov begins as soon as the previous one has departed (and sometimes earlier!). As we pack *mishloach manos* for Purim, clean for Pesach, and contemplate the arrival of Rosh Hashanah, we adapt our mood to the spirit of the upcoming holiday. Aromas of *esrogim*, cheesecake, and latkes fill the air. Preparations mount in speed and pitch as the day approaches.

As we clutch the *Sifrei Torah* and dance, gaze at the menorahs and sing, and sit on the floor to listen to *Megillas Eichah* and cry, we realize that we are not merely individuals. We are part of the great nation that is Klal Yisrael. We are members of the *Am Segulah*, Hashem's chosen nation. This is the inspiration in each Yom Tov, and this is what carries us through the year. Through celebrations and sorrows, we remember that we are Am Yisrael, Hashem's beloved ones. We recognize the love, care, and salvation Hashem has afforded us throughout the generations. And we believe that He will redeem us again, so that we may celebrate the ultimate Yom Tov in Jerusalem. May we merit it, speedily in our days.

I am grateful to Rabbi Nosson Scherman and Rabbi Meir Zlotowitz for the opportunity to work with them once again. Rabbi Scherman edited each story with the skill, care, and clarity for which he has become so well-known.

I would like to thank the entire Artscroll staff for their professionalism and expertise in preparing this book for publication. I am especially grateful to Avrohom Biderman, who smoothly blended the raw materials to produce the finished product. I also thank Mrs. Chani Stern, whose beautiful illustrations bring the lessons of the maggid alive to children.

My parents, Rabbi and Mrs. Paysach Krohn, and my parents-in-law, Mr. and Mrs. Fred Pfeiffer of Montreal, continue to be our source of inspiration, encouragement, and sound advice. They are an integral part of every aspect of our lives and accomplishments. For this, and so much more, we are forever indebted.

I would like to express my deep *hakoras hatov* to my husband, R' Shlomo Dovid, for his constant encouragement and support throughout the writing of this book. A dedicated *mechanech*, his perceptive guidance enhanced every story. May Hashem grant us Yiddishe *nachas* from our children.

I dedicate this book to the matriarch of the Pfeiffer family, Mrs. Ilse Roberg. "Oma," as she is affectionately known, personifies *hakaras hatov* and the ability to see good in every person and every situation. Her *simchas hachaim* inspired her many students, both in Stuttgart, Germany, and Detroit, as well as her family. Her beautiful artwork enhances the homes of her children and grandchildren. May Hashem give her strength to continue to be our role model and source of inspiration.

Chaviva Pfeiffer

Kew Gardens, New York
י"ד אדר א', תשס"ח

ROSH HASHANAH

GIVING AND GETTING

Avigdor and his wife Avigail lived in Teveriah, in *Eretz Yisrael*. Avigdor was happy learning Torah in the kollel there, but one thing made him and his wife very sad. They had been married many years and they still did not have children. They davened to Hashem and went to doctors, but nothing helped.

One day, Avigdor's friend said to him, "Why don't you go to the Nadvorner Rebbe, Rabbi Chaim Mordechai Rosenblum, in Bnei Brak? Maybe with the help of his *berachah*, Hashem will answer your prayer for a child."

Avigdor did not go to rebbes often, but maybe this was a good idea. He traveled to Bnei Brak and waited on line to speak to the Nadvorner Rebbe.

When his turn came, Avigdor explained his problem. He hoped the Rebbe would give him a *berachah* for a child. Instead, the Rebbe said to him, "In a

few weeks it will be Rosh Hashanah. Why don't you daven here in Bnei Brak, in my shul? On Rosh Hashanah we read from the Torah about Sarah, who did not have a child for many years, and then Hashem blessed her with Yitzchak. We also read about Chanah who did not have a child, and Hashem blessed her with a son, Shmuel. It is a *segulah* [special merit] to be called to the Torah when we read about one of those miracles. Come daven with us for Rosh Hashanah. With Hashem's help, good things can happen."

Avigdor thanked the Rebbe for his kind words. He traveled home and talked to Avigail about it. They were used to davening in their regular shul in Teveriah, but they decided to take the Rebbe's advice. They made plans to stay in Bnei Brak for Rosh Hashanah and daven with the Rebbe.

After *Maariv* on the first night of Rosh Hashanah, many people lined up to shake the Rebbe's hand and hear his *shanah tovah* blessing. Avigdor waited on the side while the many Chassidim who davened there regularly walked toward the Rebbe. As he was waiting, he saw another man also waiting patiently on the side. Avigdor went over to him and greeted him.

"Sholom Aleichem," Avigdor said warmly. "Are you also a guest?"

"Yes," answered the other man. "My name is Yisrael. I don't live here in Bnei Brak. I came here for Rosh Hashanah because my wife and I have been married many years and we have no children. The Rebbe told me that to get the *aliyah* about Chanah having a child is a *segulah* for children. I hope I will get that *aliyah* tomorrow morning, but so many people daven here ..."

Avigdor's heart sank. The *aliyah* that tells about Sarah goes to a Kohen, and Avigdor was not a Kohen. He thought, "How could the Rebbe have given the same advice to two people? Only one person will get the *aliyah*, and Yisrael is hoping it will be he."

Avigdor did not tell Yisrael that he had come to Bnei Brak for the same reason. He talked to him a while more, wished him well, and left.

That night Avigdor thought about Yisrael for a long time. He thought about how sad Yisrael must be not to have any children. He thought about how much Yisrael wanted that *aliyah*. And he made up his mind.

The next morning, Avigdor went to a different shul to daven. He found out later that Yisrael had been given the special *aliyah* in the Rebbe's shul.

However, Hashem saw that Avigdor gave up his chance so that Yisrael could get the special *aliyah*. Even though Avigdor had wanted the *aliyah* so badly, he did not tell Yisrael anything. He just davened

in a different shul so that Yisrael could have it. When a person does something so special, sometimes Hashem does something special for him. That year, Avigail had a baby girl. Just as the Rebbe had said, "Good things can happen."

When two people both want the same food, the same toy, or to talk to the same person, and only one can have it, Hashem is waiting to see: who will give in and let the other person have it? When people are kind to others, there is *shalom* (peace), which is so special to Hashem.

YOM KIPPUR

Not So Fast

Rabbi Shlomo Lorincz was a member of the Israeli Knesset (Parliament) for over thirty years. Many times questions would come up that had to be decided by a great rabbi. Rabbi Lorincz would ask Rabbi Avraham Yeshayah Karelitz, the Chazon Ish, what to do. They spoke often, and Rabbi Lorincz always followed the advice of the great *tzaddik*.

One year, a few weeks before Yom Kippur, Rabbi Lorincz became sick with a disease called typhus. He had to stay in the hospital for weeks and take a very strong medicine. Anyone taking that medicine had to eat several times a day. For days and days Rabbi Lorincz took the medicine, but Yom Kippur was just a few days away and he was not better yet.

"What if my doctor says I should eat on Yom Kippur?" Rabbi Lorincz thought. "I must fast on Yom Kippur! I can't even think about putting food into my mouth on the holiest day of the year!"

Sure enough, his doctor told him that he was still very sick, and that he must continue to take the medicine and eat a few times a day. "Can't I stop for just one day?" Rabbi Lorincz begged.

"Absolutely not," the doctor said. "Typhus is a serious illness and you must not stop taking the medicine even for one day. And it would be dangerous for you not to eat a few times each day, even on Yom Kippur."

"I must fast on Yom Kippur!" Rabbi Lorincz thought to himself. "It is a great mitzvah that I don't want to give up, even this once."

He asked his wife, "Please, ask the Chazon Ish what I should do. He will probably tell me to fast."

Mrs. Lorincz told the Chazon Ish what the doctors had said. The Chazon Ish said, "Tell your husband that I know his doctor very well and I trust him. If he says that your husband must eat on Yom Kippur, then that is what he should do."

When Rabbi Lorincz heard what the Chazon Ish said, he was shocked and saddened. How could he eat on Yom Kippur?

On the afternoon of Erev Yom Kippur, Rabbi Lorincz was lying in his hospital bed when he heard a knock at the door. "Come in," he said. He could not believe his eyes. It was the great Chazon Ish! "Maybe something happened at the Knesset that is very important," he thought. "Otherwise why would the Chazon Ish have traveled over an hour on three buses to come see me?"

The Chazon Ish said, "Your doctor says that your life will be in danger if you don't take your medicine and eat meals. I have come all the way from Bnei Brak to tell you that just as there is a mitzvah to fast on Yom Kippur, there is a mitzvah to eat if your life will be in danger."

Of course Rabbi Lorincz listened to the Chazon Ish and took his medicine and ate that Yom Kippur. He never forgot the great lesson the Chazon Ish came so far to teach him. Hashem gave us our bodies and our *neshamos* as a gift. Just as we do our best to keep our *neshamos* strong by doing mitzvos, it is also a mitzvah to keep our bodies strong by eating properly and dressing warmly in cold weather.

SUCCOS

A Big Mitzvah in a Small Place

In the 1930s, Rabbi Yoel Jakobovits and his family lived in Germany. During that time, the Jakobovitses lived in a few different apartments. Before Rabbi Jakobovits moved to a new house, he made sure there was a balcony, where he could build a succah for Succos. He also checked to be sure there was nothing over the balcony, like the balcony of a higher apartment, or the branches of a tall tree. If there is anything hanging over a succah, the succah is not kosher (fit for use).

In those years, the Germans were very mean to the Jews. If they saw a Jew doing a mitzvah, they might beat him up or take him to jail. Most Jews tried to do mitzvos inside their homes, where the Germans would not see them.

It was almost Succos of 1938. Rabbi Jakobovits stood in his third-floor apartment and looked at his balcony. "What will happen to my family if I build a succah this year?" he thought. "Will the Germans try to harm us?"

Then he had an idea. He got a ruler and went out onto the balcony. He measured the walls of the balcony. They were forty-four inches high. Short, but not too short. "I will build a succah with very short walls!" he told his children, Shlomo and Immanuel. "Even a succah with walls that are ten *tefachim* [forty inches] high is a kosher succah. We can sit inside the succah, and no one down on the street will see us, because the walls of the balcony will hide the sides of the succah!"

"But how will we sit in such a tiny succah?" the children asked.

"You will see," their father said. "When you really want to do a mitzvah, you always find a way."

When Succos came, the Jakobovitses crawled into their succah. They ate all their meals sitting on pillows instead of chairs. For the rest of their lives, Shlomo and Immanuel remembered and told their children about the *mesiras nefesh* (self-sacrifice) of their grandfather, Rabbi Yoel Jakobovits, to fulfill the mitzvah of succah.

CHANUKAH

Seeing the Point

Mr. Aryeh Leib Hilvicht was a wealthy Jew who lived in Milan, Italy, over one hundred years ago. Anyone who needed a Shabbos meal knew he could come to the Hilvicht home. Mr. Hilvicht enjoyed having all kinds of people at his Shabbos table.

One Shabbos, a man from Yerushalayim named Reb Lipa was among the guests. As Reb Lipa looked around the dining room, he noticed a breakfront full of expensive objects. He had never seen so much gold and silver in one home. Only one thing seemed out of place. On the middle shelf sat a broken jar. Sharp points stuck out of it all around the top. "There must be something special about that broken jar," thought Reb Lipa, "otherwise it would not be in the breakfront with all the gold and silver."

Mr. Hilvicht saw that Reb Lipa was looking at something. "Is everything all right?" he asked him.

"Oh, yes," answered Reb Lipa. "I was just wondering about that broken jar. It seems so out of place in the breakfront. There must be a reason why you keep it there."

Mr. Hilvicht smiled. He enjoyed telling the story of the jar. "Yes," he said, "there is a reason. It is because of something that happened to me many years ago." And he began to tell the story of his life.

"I grew up in Amsterdam. When I was eighteen years old, my grandfather, who lived here in Italy, asked me to come help him in his store. I came, and I enjoyed working in the store very much. When my grandfather passed away, I asked my parents if I could stay in Italy. They said yes, and I became busier than ever. All day long I worked in the store with customers and merchandise. Soon I was a rich man.

"One day, I was so busy, I forgot to daven *Minchah*. A few days later I skipped *Shacharis*. I told myself, 'Tomorrow I'll make sure to daven.' But I didn't. One by one, I stopped keeping all the mitzvos. I married and had a family, but Torah and *Yiddishkeit* [Judaism] were no longer part of my life.

"One evening, as I was walking home from work, I saw some children playing happily. Suddenly, one boy started crying. The others crowded around him, trying to calm him down, but nothing could cheer him up. I could hear him crying, 'What will I tell my father? What will I tell my father?'

"I bent over and asked him, 'What is the matter?'

"Between sobs he answered, 'My father has been saving up money for months to buy some oil for the Chanukah menorah. Today he gave me the money and told me to go to the store and buy a small bottle of oil. He warned me to come straight home so that the bottle would not break. I bought the oil, but on my way home I saw my friends playing. I stopped to play for just a few minutes. While we were playing the bottle fell over and broke. My father will be so upset with me. What will I tell him when I come home?' And he started crying all over again.

"'Please don't cry,' I told him. I gave him a lot of money and told him to go right back to the store and buy a *big* bottle of oil for his father. He was so happy.

"Then I bent down and picked up the pieces of the broken bottle. I held them in my hands and looked at them. 'What will *I* tell *my* Father?' I thought to myself. 'After my life ends, what will I tell Hashem, my Father in Heaven?' I had strayed so far from *Yiddishkeit* that I didn't even know Chanukah was about to begin. I decided to buy myself a bottle of oil, too, and light a menorah that night.

"I went home and told my wife and children all about Chanukah. We lit one flame that night. The next night we lit two flames, and the next night three. Little by little, I taught my family about the beautiful mitzvos in the Torah. We began to keep Shabbos, eat kosher food, and celebrate all the *Yomim Tovim*. My life became special once again, all because of that broken bottle and the little boy's words, 'What will I tell my father?'

"Now you see," said Mr. Hilvicht to Reb Lipa, "why I keep that broken jar together with all my gold and silver. It is one of the most precious things I own, because it brought me back to the ways of the Torah."

Every person makes mistakes. We are not perfect. Hopefully, we are wise enough, as Mr. Hilvicht was, to understand when Hashem is trying to show us that it is time to fix our ways and become better.

TU B'SHVAT

BAGGED

Reb Shepsil Gutfarb and his wife Chaya live in Yerushalayim. He is a rebbe in a yeshivah.

One day, Reb Shepsil came home after class. He was hungry and wanted something to eat. He opened the refrigerator.

"Chaya," he said, "Are there any apples left? I think there were two here this morning."

"I gave the two apples to the Arab *ozeret* [cleaning lady]," answered Chaya. "She just left a few minutes ago, and she said she was hungry, so I gave her the two apples to eat on the bus."

"Oy vey!" shouted Reb Shepsil. "Those were *peiros shvi'is*!" *Peiros shvi'is* are fruits that grow during *Shemittah*, the seventh year, when farmers in *Eretz Yisrael* may not work the ground. Any fruits that grow have special *kedushah* [holiness]. There are many special laws about *peiros shvi'is*. They must be cared for in special ways, and the *ozeret* would not care for them properly!

"I must run to the bus stop and see if I can find the *ozeret* and get the apples back," said Reb Shepsil as he dashed out the door.

When he got to the bus stop, the *ozeret* was not there.

"Did a bus just leave?" he asked the people waiting.

"A bus left ten minutes ago," a man answered.

Reb Shepsil knew where the *ozeret* would get off the bus to transfer to a second bus that would take her home. He hired a taxi to take him to that bus stop.

When he got to the bus stop, he saw the *ozeret*'s second bus waiting. "Maybe she is on that bus," he thought. He stepped up onto the bus and said to the driver, "I am looking for someone. Do you mind if I check to see if she is on this bus? I will get right off when I am done." The driver said it was fine.

Reb Shepsil walked down the aisle of the bus quickly, looking on both sides for the *ozeret*. He finally found her near the back.

With great excitement he said to her, "*Eifoh hasakit*? *Eifoh hasakit*? [Where is the bag? Where is the bag?]"

The *ozeret* seemed very frightened. She said, "Don't call the police! Please, don't call the police!" Then she handed Reb Shepsil a small bag. Inside were a necklace, two bracelets, and a pair of earrings that she had stolen from Mrs. Gutfarb. Mrs. Gutfarb had not yet looked for them, so she had not even noticed that they were missing! Only because Reb Shepsil was so careful to keep the mitzvah of *shvi'is* was he able to get back his wife's jewelry.

And, of course, he got back the apples, too.

PURIM

Knot for Purim

Rav Pinchos had been a beloved Rosh Yeshivah for many years. His talmidim loved him and always treated him with great respect. But there was one day of the year when the boys sang songs and put on plays that joked about the Rosh Yeshivah and the yeshivah itself. That day was Purim.

The Rosh Yeshivah did not mind. When the boys were finished with their song about him, he would make up a joking song and sing it to them right then. Everyone had a good time.

There was another joke that some of the boys would play on the Rosh Yeshivah every year. After the Megillah reading on Purim night, they would go into Rav Pinchos's office and find his tefillin. Tefillin have a special knot, which is called a *kesher*. There are different types of knots. The Rosh Yeshivah's tefillin were tied with an Ashkenaz knot. The boys would untie the knot, and retie it the Sefard way. The next morning, on Purim day, the Rosh Yeshivah would switch the knot back to Ashkenaz and walk into the beis hamidrash with a big smile on his face.

This went on year after year. The boys had fun, and the Rosh Yeshivah did not seem to mind. Some years Rav Pinchos tried to hide his tefillin, but each year the boys found them and changed the knot. And every year the Rosh Yeshivah changed the knot back and came into the beis hamidrash smiling.

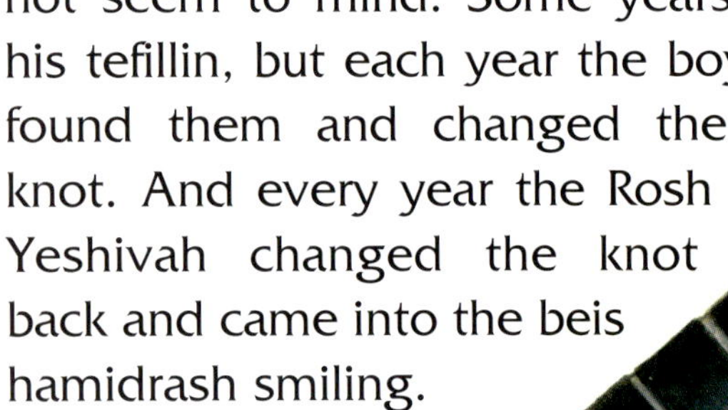

One year a new boy came to the yeshivah, and he joined the group that pulled the prank. That year, instead of the boy who usually changed the knot, the new boy was the one who redid the knot. That Purim, when Rav Pinchos came to yeshivah in the morning and found the knot switched, he could not get it open. He tried for five minutes, ten minutes, even twenty minutes, but it was tied so tightly that he could not open it. No matter how hard he tried, Rav Pinchos could not untie the knot. As he kept trying, he heard that the boys were almost finished davening, and he had missed davening with a minyan. The Rosh Yeshivah was so upset! How could he have missed davening with a minyan, especially on Purim?

The rest of the day, everyone could see that the Rosh Yeshivah was very sad. "How could my talmidim make the knot so tight that it is impossible to open?" he thought. Not only did he miss davening with a minyan, but the *retzuos* (straps) of the tefillin had to be cut so that he could make a new *kesher*.

On Friday night, when the Rosh Yeshivah spoke to the entire yeshivah, he said, "What happened on Purim was very wrong. Whoever tightened the knot on my tefillin so tightly that I missed davening with a minyan must ask for *mechilah* [forgiveness]. I can only forgive the boy if he comes to me."

Days and weeks passed. Nobody came to ask the Rosh Yeshivah for *mechilah*. Over the summer most people forgot about it, but before Yom Kippur the Rosh Yeshivah talked about it again. "I still remember what happened on Purim," he said. "The boy who made me miss davening with a minyan must ask for *mechilah* before Yom Kippur, otherwise I cannot forgive him and Hashem cannot forgive him." Again, nobody came to ask the Rosh Yeshivah for forgiveness.

Soon after that, the boy who usually changed the knot switched yeshivos. No one ever talked to him about the tefillin. The next year, a few days before Purim, a man in shul asked him, "Can you please help me tie the knot on my tefillin? It opened up and I don't know how to tie it." The boy helped him.

The next year, in a different city, on the day after Purim, a thirteen-year-old boy in shul said to him, "My tefillin *shel rosh* [tefillin of the head] is too loose. Do you know how to make the knot tighter?" The boy helped him.

The third year, in a different shul, on Purim, an older man was having trouble with his tefillin. He turned to the boy and said, "Can you help me with my tefillin?" As he fixed the knot, the boy suddenly thought to himself, "Why doesn't anyone ever ask me about tefillin all year long? Only around Purim time do people ask me to help them with their tefillin. Could it have something to do with what I did to Rav Pinchos on Purim a few years ago?" It bothered him, but he tried not to think about it.

The fourth year, as Purim came closer, he wondered if anyone would ask him about tefillin. Sure enough, on Purim, a man asked for help with the knot of his tefillin. With fear in his heart, he fixed the knot. He knew that he was the one who had usually changed the knot of his Rosh Yeshivah's tefillin. Even though he had not done it that last year, maybe the Rosh Yeshivah suspected him, for good reason. But what could he do now? He was very far from his old yeshivah. He called a friend of his who was still there, and told him what had been happening. "Please," he begged him, "go to Rav Pinchos and tell him truthfully that I did not do it. Ask him to be *mochel* me if I caused him to be upset."

After that, no one ever asked him for help with tefillin again.

Many, many years have passed. Now this boy is an old man. When he talks about the story, he says, "Since it was the new boy who made the knot so tight that year, I did not ask the Rosh Yeshivah for *mechilah*. But I should have gone to the Rosh Yeshivah anyway, because I realized later that he was upset with me. I also learned that a mean joke is never funny, not even on Purim."

PESACH

The Rebbe's Matzos

After World War II ended, many Jews in Europe could not return to their homes. In the city of Chernovitz, which was then part of Russia, the Sekulener Rebbe and many other Chassidic rebbes and their Chassidim waited to leave Europe and travel to a safer place.

It was a few weeks before Pesach, and the Sekulener Rebbe realized that the only way that they would have matzos was if he would bake them himself. He sent a Chassid to a nearby farm to buy wheat. Then the Rebbe and his Chassidim carefully ground the wheat into flour, mixed it with water, and baked as many matzos as they could.

Because the Sekulener Rebbe could get only a small amount of wheat, there were not enough matzos for everyone. He decided to give only three matzos to each of the great rabbis in the city. He sent his Chassidim to deliver them.

Soon after the matzos were baked, Rabbi Baruch Hager, the Seret-Vizhnitzer Rebbe, sent his son Reb Moshe to the Sekulener Rebbe. "May I please have matzos for my father?" he asked.

"Of course." replied the Sekulener Rebbe. "It would be an honor to give you matzos for your father." With great joy he handed Reb Moshe three matzos.

"I am sorry," said Reb Moshe softly. "My father asked me to bring him six matzos."

"Six matzos?" asked the Sekulener Rebbe. "How can I give you six matzos? We barely have enough to give everyone three! I didn't give anyone six matzos."

"What can I do?" answered Reb Moshe. "My father told me not to leave until I have exactly six matzos. How can I go against the mitzvah of *kibbud av* [honoring one's father]?"

The Sekulener Rebbe felt he had no choice. He gave Reb Moshe three more matzos and wished him a *chag kosher v'samei'ach.* Reb Moshe happily brought the matzos home to his father.

On Erev Pesach, Reb Moshe came back holding three matzos. "My father said I should bring you these three matzos." he told the Sekulener Rebbe.

The Sekulener Rebbe could not believe what he was hearing, "Now you bring me the matzos?" he said. "I wanted to give you only three to begin with. Why did your father ask me for six if he really only wanted three?"

Reb Moshe answered, "My father told me, 'The Sekulener Rebbe is such a kind person, he will probably give away every single matzah he has and not leave any for himself.' My father asked for six matzos so that today, on Erev Pesach, he could send you back three matzos, and you will have matzah for your own seder."

Reb Baruch Hager was right. The Sekulener Rebbe had given away all the matzos that he had baked. The only matzos he had at his seder were the matzos that Reb Baruch sent him that day.

This story shows us how much our great rabbis care for others. The Sekulener Rebbe worked to bake matzos and give them away to others, and the Seret-Vizhnitzer Rebbe made sure that the Sekulener Rebbe would have matzos for himself. Let us learn from the ways of our *gedolim* to think of others and care for their needs as much as we do for ourselves.

SHAVUOS

Heartwarming

Rabbi Yaakov Dovid Wilavsky was the Rav of Tzefas, in *Eretz Yisrael*. Once when he had *Yahrzeit*, he sat next to the furnace in his shul and cried bitterly. The people asked him why he was crying. He told them this story.

Yaakov Dovid Wilavsky grew up in Kobrin, a small town in Belarus. He was such a bright boy that his parents wanted him to have extra learning. They hired a very good *melamed* (private teacher) named Reb Chaim Sender. Reb Chaim charged one ruble a month, which was a lot of money for the Wilavskys, but they wanted the best for Yaakov Dovid.

Reb Zev Wilavsky earned a living by making furnaces for people. A furnace was very important, because people would use it as an oven to cook their food and also to heat their homes.

One winter, Reb Zev could not make money, because it was very hard to find cement and lime. Without cement and lime, it is impossible to build a furnace. He could not afford to pay Reb Chaim!

Three months went by, and still Reb Chaim had not been paid. Finally, he sent Reb Zev a note. If he was not paid the next day, he could not keep teaching Yaakov Dovid, because he needed money to support his family.

Reb Zev and his wife did not know what to do. They wanted Yaakov Dovid to become a big *talmid chacham*. What could be more important than that? They *had* to find a way to pay Reb Chaim! But how?

That night Reb Zev went to shul for *Maariv*. He heard a wealthy man say, "My son is getting married soon, and the men building his new house cannot get a furnace anywhere! My son must have a new furnace for his house. What can I do? I will pay six rubles to anyone who can build one for me."

Reb Zev had an idea. He went home and talked about it with his wife. They decided that Reb Zev would take apart his own furnace, brick by brick, and use the parts to build a nice new one for the rich man's son. They knew it would be a hard winter for them without a furnace, but the most important thing was that Yaakov Dovid learn Torah every day with his wonderful *melamed*. They told Reb Chaim what they were doing, and he did not miss a single day of learning with Yaakov Dovid.

When Reb Zev finished building the furnace, the rich man paid him six rubles. Reb Zev gave all the money to Yaakov Dovid and said, "I am so proud of how well you are learning. Your mother and I want you to continue learning with your *melamed* every day. Please give this money to Reb Chaim." Reb Zev wrote a note to Reb Chaim that the extra money was for the next three months.

That winter was very hard for the Wilavsky family. Many days they were freezing cold. But they did not mind. It was more important to them that their Yaakov Dovid could learn Torah with the best *melamed* in town.

Yaakov Dovid continued to learn Torah for many more years. He became a Rav in Slutzk, Poland, and later in Tzefas in *Eretz Yisrael*. He was known

as the Ridvaz, the name of his famous *peirush* (commentary) on the Talmud Yerushalmi. Even when he was very old, the Ridvaz thought of his parents on cold winter days. He knew that he had become such a great *talmid chacham* because his parents had given up so much for his Torah learning.

SHABBOS

Wheels of Wonder

Sam Zeitlin loved to ride his bicycle. As he grew up, he spent many hours practicing to ride as fast as he could. Many times he would race his friends and win.

When he was old enough, Sam joined the American National Cycling Team. He was in races all over the United States. Everyone knew that Sam Zeitlin was one of the best cyclists in America. Maybe he would even race in the Olympics.

There was only one problem. Some of the other cyclists did not like Sam. They would yell at him and call him names. One of them even tried to hurt him. Sam knew that they were doing this for only one reason: because he was Jewish.

Sam was not a religious Jew. He did not know about Shabbos or davening. But these others did not care. They hated him anyway.

Sam felt that in America he would never make it to the Olympics. The other cyclists would make sure of that. Sam knew that *Eretz Yisrael* was the Land of his people. And if he could not stay in America, he would go there.

When Sam arrived in Israel, he met with Nati, the manager of the Israeli cycling team. "If you let me join your team," Sam said, "I will help train your cyclists so well, they may even get to race in the Olympics."

Israel had never sent a cycling team to the Olympics. Its cyclists were not good enough. But Nati had heard of Sam. Everyone knew how good Sam was. "I would be happy to have you join our team," Nati told him.

Sam started practicing right away. He was a great help to the team.

Meanwhile, Sam also toured the country. One day he went to the *Kosel Hamaaravi*. He saw that everyone was davening. Sam whispered the only prayer he knew, "*Shema Yisrael Hashem Elokeinu Hashem Echad.*" Then he looked around. "What is everyone saying?" he thought to himself. "I wish I knew more prayers."

Someone told Sam about Rabbi Gershon Weinberger. Many Jewish young men and women who wanted to learn more about *Yiddishkeit* (Judaism) came to Rabbi Weinberger. Sam loved to learn with him and be his Shabbos guest. He loved to sing *zemiros* and listen to *divrei Torah*. Sam started to use his Hebrew name, Shimon.

One day Rabbi Weinberger said, "Shimon, let me tell you about a place where you can learn much more than here in my home. Rabbi Noach Weinberg has opened a new yeshivah in Bnei Brak called Yeshivah Magen Avraham. He will answer all your questions and teach you as much as you want. It is the perfect place for you."

Shimon went to Bnei Brak, to Yeshivah Magen Avraham. He learned there every morning. In the afternoons he would ride his bicycle for hours in and around Bnei Brak. Here there were no hills, as there were in Yerushalayim, and there was almost no wind. As he rode, Shimon thought about how exciting it would be to finally make it to the Olympics, and he would sing *Shabbos HaYom Lashem*, which he had learned at Rabbi Weinberger's Shabbos table. It was a quick tune that kept his feet pedaling speedily, mile after mile.

As time went on, Shimon became more and more excited. The time for the Olympic try-outs was nearing. He waited each day to hear the exact time and place. And then the announcement came. The tryouts would be held on Shabbos! Shimon's heart sank. How could the Israeli sports team schedule tryouts for Shabbos? He begged them to let him try out on a different day, but they refused. "We don't make exceptions for anyone," they told him. "Not even for you."

By now Shimon had begun keeping Shabbos. Trying out on Shabbos was out of the question. He tried not to think about the thousands of hours he had spent training, lifting weights, and cycling on hot summer afternoons and cold, rainy winter days to prepare for the Olympics. But Shabbos was more important to him than the chance to win a medal. He would not try out for the team.

That year, 1972, Israel sent eleven athletes to the Olympic games, which were held in Germany. The country did not send any cyclists.

During the games, a group of Arabs attacked the apartments where the Israeli athletes were staying. All eleven were murdered.

Jews around the world were shocked and saddened. How could such a terrible tragedy happen at the Olympic games? Shimon shuddered when he thought of another Shabbos song, "*Ki Eshmerah Shabbos, Keil Yishmarayni — If I keep Shabbos, Hashem will protect me.*" He felt that his life had been saved because he kept Shabbos.

For the rest of his life, Shimon thanked Hashem as he sang this song at his Shabbos table with his family. "*Baruch Hashem*, I keep Shabbos," he thought to himself.

SHABBOS

Shabbos Rest

The Tchebiner Rav, Rabbi Dov Berish Weidenfeld, lived in Yerushalayim from 1946 until he passed away in 1965. He was a very great *talmid chacham* and people always came to ask him questions about Torah or to seek his advice. He was usually up late at night, either learning Torah or speaking to people.

One Shabbos afternoon, after the Rav had finished his Shabbos meal, he was very tired. He went to lie down and rest for a while. Just as the Rav began to rest, he heard a knock at the door.

"Oy, I am so tired," thought the Rav. "Maybe the person will come back later."

But then there was a second knock, and a third. "Maybe it is important," he thought. "If someone needs my help, I must answer the door." The Rav got up and went to the door.

When Reb Dov Berish opened the door, he was surprised to see a nine-year-old boy named Yankele, holding a *gemara*! "Can I help you?" the Rav asked.

"Yes," said Yankele. "I just finished learning some *gemara* in yeshivah. Can the Rav please test me?"

"Of course," said the Rav. "Come in and sit down."

Yankele sat down and opened his *gemara*. Then the Rav said, "I will be happy to listen to you read, but first let me explain something to you. If you knock on someone's door on Shabbos afternoon and there is no answer, and you knock again and there is still no answer, you should think, 'Maybe the person is resting.'"

Yankele's face turned pale. He could not believe what he was hearing. "I ... I didn't think a Rav sleeps on Shabbos," he said softly.

The Rav thought about what Yankele said. "This boy thinks a Rav spends the whole Shabbos learning or answering people's questions. Maybe that is really what I should be doing. Maybe I should not rest on Shabbos afternoon!"

From that day on, the Tchebiner Rav did not rest on Shabbos afternoon. He took Yankele's lesson to heart, even though Yankele was a child.

We can also learn from people younger from us. We can learn from small children how to say *berachos* slowly and clearly. Many small children say *Shema* every night, and go right to sleep when they are told to. Even if someone is younger than us, we can learn good things from him, just as the Tchebiner Rav learned from a nine-year-old boy.

SHABBOS

Holding on Tight

Jacobo Sherem lives in Mexico City with his wife and family. His business is buying and selling office buildings.

For many years, Jacobo did not know much about *Yiddishkeit* (Judaism). Then he started going to classes a few nights a week to learn about Shabbos, eating kosher, and keeping other Jewish laws. Over time, Jacobo became more and more religious. He started going to shul on Friday nights, and then began to keep his business closed on Shabbos.

One Friday, two men came to see him. They wanted to buy one of his buildings. It was a big building with many offices in it. Jacobo would make a lot of money if he sold them the building.

Jacobo showed the men through the building. They went from floor to floor, looking at every single office. Then they sat down to talk. The men had many questions. They talked about what each office could be used for, how much they would have to pay for the building, and when they would have to pay the money.

All this time, Jacobo kept looking at his watch. It was Friday, only a few hours until Shabbos. How long could he stay here with these men? He had to go home and get ready for Shabbos. He tried to rush the men, but everything seemed to take so long.

Now it was only an hour and a half before Shabbos. Jacobo finally told the men, "I am very sorry, but I cannot continue to talk to you today. I must go home now."

The men said, "But we are leaving Mexico tomorrow to fly to a different country. Please stay longer so we can finish talking. We are ready to pay you a good price for the building. But if you go home now, we will not buy it."

Jacobo said, "I don't care if I give up a lot of money. It is late and I must leave now. It was nice meeting you."

They shook hands and parted. The next day the men left Mexico. Jacobo wished he could have sold them the building, but Shabbos was more important to him than money.

About two weeks later, a big earthquake shook the ground in Mexico City. Many houses and office buildings fell. Many people were hurt. Downtown Mexico City was a mess. On one block, every building had fallen ... except Jacobo's.

Over the next few days, many people called Jacobo. They needed office space and they wanted to buy his building. Important people from the government called. "Can we buy your building? Ours collapsed in the earthquake. We need office space right away. We will pay you as much money as you want."

Other people called. "Part of our building was damaged. Can we buy some of the offices in your building? We will pay anything. We need offices!"

The phone rang again. "I hear you have offices for sale. I cannot work in my office because the whole building is in danger of falling. I want to buy a whole floor of your building. Just tell me how much to pay. I will bring you the money right now!"

Jacobo sold all the offices in his building that week. He made a fortune — much more than he would have if he had sold the building to the two men who had come to him that Friday.

Jacobo told his friends, "Look how Hashem rewarded me for keeping Shabbos so carefully. At first I thought I was giving up so much for *Shmiras Shabbos* [keeping Shabbos], but now I see that I got so much because of my *Shmiras Shabbos*."

The reward Hashem gives us for keeping His mitzvos is greater than we can imagine.

When Great Men "Disagree"

Shaya Goldberg studied in Yeshivas Ner Yisrael in Baltimore. He was very close to the Rosh Yeshivah, Rabbi Yaakov Yitzchak Ruderman.

When Shaya became engaged to be married, he rushed to tell Rabbi Ruderman the good news and when the wedding would take place. Then he said, "Would the Rosh Yeshivah please be the *mesader kiddushin* [one who performs the wedding ceremony]?"

Rabbi Ruderman said, "I am very sorry, Shaya. I would love to come to your wedding, but I must be in a different city that night."

Shaya was disappointed, but he understood. The Rosh Yeshivah was a very important man. Many people needed his help.

When Shaya's father heard that Rabbi Ruderman could not make it, he thought to himself, "The *gadol hador* [greatest rabbi of the generation], Rabbi Moshe Feinstein, lives in our apartment building. Wouldn't it be wonderful if Reb Moshe could be the *mesader kiddushin* at Shaya's wedding?" Shaya, too, thought it was a wonderful idea.

Mr. Goldberg went to visit Reb Moshe. He explained that Shaya's Rosh Yeshivah could not be the *mesader kiddushin*, and asked if Reb Moshe would do it instead. Reb Moshe said, "The rebbetzin and I would be happy to come to Shaya's wedding. If you want me to, I will be the *mesader kiddushin*."

A few days before the wedding, Rabbi Ruderman told Shaya happily, "My plans have changed. I will be able to come to your wedding after all!"

Shaya was thrilled. When he went home for Shabbos, he told his father the good news. "But, Shaya," his father said, "when you told me that Rabbi Ruderman could not make it, I asked Rabbi Moshe Feinstein to be the *mesader kiddushin*. He is the *gadol hador*! How can I tell him that we changed our minds and we don't want him to be the *mesader kiddushin*?"

Shaya and Mr. Goldberg did not know what to do. They decided to go to Reb Moshe together and explain the problem. But what would they say?

They went to Reb Moshe's apartment and knocked on the door. They didn't have to say one word. As soon as Reb Moshe looked at their faces, he said, "I am coming to your wedding as a neighbor and a friend. I am not coming because I want to have an honor. Even if someone else will be the *mesader kiddushin*, it will be my pleasure to come."

Mr. Goldberg and Shaya were amazed that Reb Moshe understood the problem even before they opened their mouths. They were also proud that Reb Moshe and Rabbi Ruderman would both come to the wedding.

On the night of the wedding, both great rabbis were there. When Rabbi Ruderman saw Reb Moshe, he said, "I did not know that you would be here! Of course, you will be the *mesader kiddushin*. You are the *mara d'asra* [leader of the community]!"

Reb Moshe answered, "Oh, no. You are Shaya's Rosh Yeshivah, so the honor is yours."

Each rabbi tried to convince the other to accept the honor. Finally, Rabbi Ruderman thought of something. "You are older," he told Reb Moshe. "So surely you should be the *mesader kiddushin*!" He was sure Reb Moshe would not have a better answer than that.

Reb Moshe nodded his head. "Yes, I am older. That means you have to listen to me. And I am asking you to be the *mesader kiddushin*."

So Rabbi Ruderman was the *mesader kiddushin*, and Reb Moshe read the *kesubah*, which is also a great honor.

The people who overheard their conversation learned something very important. Instead of taking the honor for himself, each Rav tried to give the other one the honor.

When only one person can have something, let us not take it for ourselves. Instead, let us try to act like these great rabbis and give the honor, or the toy, or the food to someone else.

The Tenth Man

It was during the First World War, in 1917, when the hated Russian czar had been overthrown.

Mendel was one of the many Jews in Russia who bought and sold jewelry for a living. Every morning Mendel would be in his office at 8:00, and spend his day meeting with customers and other diamond dealers. Business was going very well.

One morning, Mendel was on his way to work. As usual, he was carrying his small briefcase of jewelry. As he walked down the street, a man named Velvel, whom he did not know, called out from the doorway of a small shul, "Reb Yid!" Mendel turned around. "Please," Velvel continued, "I have *yahrzheit* today for my father. I need a minyan [ten men] so I can say *Kaddish.* Won't you please come inside and join us?"

Mendel looked at his watch. It was still early. "Yes," he answered. "I will join your minyan."

To Mendel's surprise there were only four other men there. "What's this?" he asked Velvel. "I am only the fifth one! How will you ever find five more?"

"Don't worry," Velvel answered. "Many Jewish people pass by on their way to work. We will have ten men very soon."

Mendel was not too happy, but he agreed to wait. He sat down and started to say *Tehillim.*

Soon Mendel looked at his watch again. It was exactly 8:00, and only two more men had come.

"Please let me leave," Mendel said to Velvel. "I am late for work and we still only have seven people."

"Absolutely not," Velvel answered. "I must say *Kaddish* today and I will not let you leave until we have a minyan."

Mendel tried to argue but he saw it was no use, so he sat back down and said some more *Tehillim.* Another ten minutes passed. Only two more people had come. By now Mendel was very upset. He started walking to the door to leave, but Velvel stopped him. "If *you* needed a minyan, you would not want anyone to leave, right? You will stay until we have a minyan*!*"

Mendel saw that he had no choice. Velvel was right. He waited and waited

until finally, at 8:30, a tenth man came. Mendel thought Velvel would just say *Kaddish* and let him go, but instead he started davening from the beginning of *Shacharis.* Mendel looked at his watch again. "At this rate, I won't get to my office until 9:30!" he thought to himself.

When Velvel finally finished davening, Mendel rushed out. Quickly, he walked down the streets to his office. When he was about two blocks from his office, he saw a friend running toward him, waving his hands wildly. "Quick, run for your life!" he screamed to Mendel. "The Communists took over the government today. They came to the diamond shops looking for Jews to rob! They are beating up Jews and stealing their diamonds and jewelry! Get away as fast as you can!"

Mendel turned around and ran. He hid for a few days, until it was safe to come out. A few months later he was able to leave Russia and move to *Eretz Yisrael*. There he did not have to worry about Communists who chased Jews.

If Mendel had gone to work any earlier, his life would have been in real danger. He was sure that Hashem had saved his life because he stayed in shul to be part of Velvel's minyan. Mendel realized that Hashem rewards us for every mitzvah we do.

The Necklace

Mr. and Mrs. Yehuda Hoffner lived in London, England. One night, they went to a wedding. Late at night, near the end of the wedding, Mr. and Mrs. Hoffner were ready to go home. Suddenly, Mrs. Hoffner noticed something sparkling on the floor. She bent down and picked it up. It was a beautiful gold necklace, studded with diamonds. But whose was it? One of the guests at the wedding must have lost it.

Mrs. Hoffner went to the manager of the wedding hall to tell him about it. He announced for everyone to hear, "If any woman lost an expensive piece of jewelry, please come to my office." But nobody came.

"I guess the owner of the necklace left already," Mrs. Hoffner told her husband. "Now how will I find out who lost it? I must return this necklace to its owner."

"Let's tell the parents of the chassan and kallah about it," he suggested. "Maybe they can help us."

So they went to the parents of the chassan and kallah. But none of them knew who had lost the necklace. "If anyone calls you and tells you they lost a necklace, please give them my number," said Mrs. Hoffner.

A few days went by. Nobody called. "Let us ask Rabbi Henoch Padwa what to do," Mr. Hoffner told his wife. "He is one of the great rabbis of London. He will know what we should do."

Rabbi Padwa said, "Hang up signs in the shuls saying, 'An expensive item was found at a wedding. If you think it is yours, please call the Hoffners.' You should also wear the necklace to every wedding you go to," he told Mrs. Hoffner. "Maybe someone will see it and recognize it."

The Hoffners did everything Rabbi Padwa said. Still, no one called and no one recognized the necklace. After a few months, Mrs. Hoffner stopped wearing the necklace. She put it in a safe place and for almost ten years, that is where it stayed.

One day Mrs. Hoffner heard sad news. Rabbi Padwa had passed away. Then Mrs. Hoffner remembered that she had once asked Rabbi Padwa about the necklace. She was planning to go to a wedding a few weeks later. "I have not worn that necklace in many years," she thought. "Maybe if I wear the necklace to the wedding, someone will recognize it."

The night of the wedding, Mrs. Hoffner carefully took the necklace out of its safe place. She rubbed it with a dry cloth until it sparkled the way it had the night she found it. Then she put it on.

At the wedding, Mrs. Hoffner saw many people. When she was dancing, a woman she did not know started talking to her. She was from Israel, and had come to London for this wedding. All at once, the woman said to Mrs. Hoffner, "The necklace you are wearing is so beautiful. I used to have one just like it. I came to London about ten years ago for a wedding, and when I was packing to go back home, I could not find it. It has been missing all these years."

Mrs. Hoffner could not believe her ears. "You are not going to believe this," she told the woman, "but this is your necklace! I found it at a wedding here in London about ten years ago, and I have been searching for the owner. I had the manager announce it at the wedding, I put up signs in shul, and a Rav told me to wear it to weddings to see if anyone would recognize it. I wore it to a few weddings; then I put it away until tonight. Now I understand why I could not find the owner. You were back in Israel. I am so happy to be able to do the mitzvah of *hashavas aveidah* [returning a lost item]." Mrs. Hoffner took off the necklace and gave it to the woman.

She was thrilled. "Thank you, thank you! I finally have my precious necklace back! You are so kind to try so hard to find me, and to keep it all these years.

By the way, if you have not worn the necklace all these years, what made you wear it tonight?"

"Rabbi Padwa was the one who told me to wear the necklace," answered Mrs. Hoffner. "When I heard that he passed away, I remembered what he told me then. I decided to wear it the next time I could, and that is tonight!"

This story shows us how important it is to listen to the words of our rabbis. When Mrs. Hoffner followed the words of Rabbi Padwa, she was finally able to do the mitzvah of *hashavas aveidah*.

Greetings

Izzy Nachmal owns a kosher slaughterhouse in Argentina, South America. A slaughterhouse is where cows and other animals are *shechted* (slaughtered according to *halachah*) so Jewish people can eat their meat.

About two hundred people work there every day. In the morning, the guard, Domingo, watches the workers come in. He stands near the front gate all day to make sure only workers come in and out. At the end of the day, Domingo watches as the workers leave one by one to go home.

Mr. Nachmal usually is the last one to leave. One evening, as he was leaving, he told Domingo as usual, "You can lock up now and go home, Domingo. Everyone has left."

"Excuse me, sir," Domingo answered. "Rabbi Berkowitz has not left yet."

"Are you sure?" Mr. Nachmal answered. "Maybe he left and you didn't notice."

"I am sure," said Domingo.

Domingo and Mr. Nachmal searched the building for Rabbi Berkowitz. "Maybe he became ill and fainted while he was changing his clothes in the dressing room," said Domingo. But he was not in the dressing room.

"Let's check the business office," said Mr. Nachmal. But Rabbi Berkowitz was not there either. Now they were beginning to worry. Where could he be? They ran from room to room, but they could not find him.

Finally, they opened the door to the huge refrigerator, where the meat was kept before it was sent to the stores. To their surprise, there was Rabbi Berkowitz! He was half-frozen, and was rolling on the floor, trying to keep warm. They took him out quickly and covered him with blankets to warm him up. Mr. Nachmal rushed to make him a cup of hot tea.

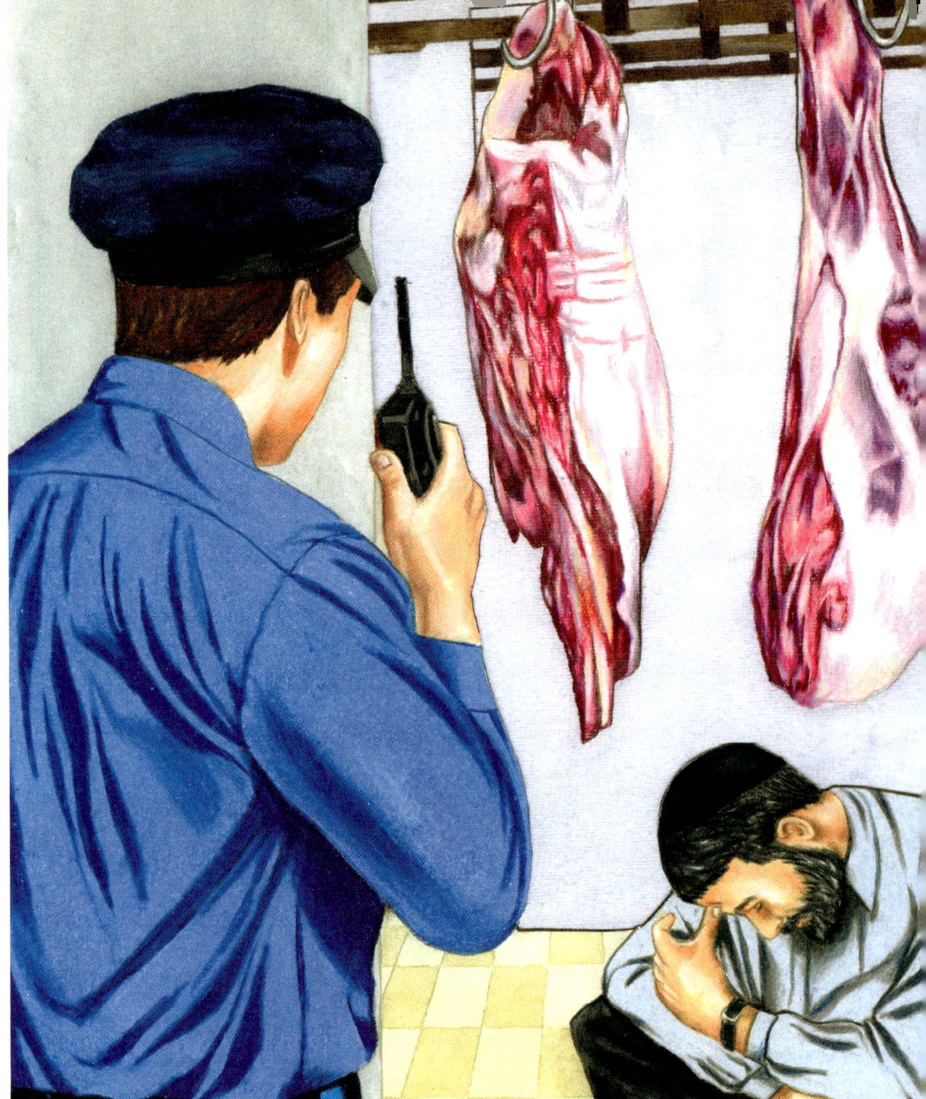

"What happened?" Mr. Nachmal asked Rabbi Berkowitz.

Rabbi Berkowitz's teeth were chattering. He answered, "When I was putting some meat into the refrigerator, the door closed behind me. The handle inside was stuck, and as hard as I pushed, it wouldn't open the door. I was locked inside! I don't know how much longer I could have lasted in there. Thank you so much for saving my life!"

"Well," Mr. Nachmal said, "You really have to thank Domingo. I told him to lock up and go home, but he insisted that you were still inside. We searched and searched until we found you."

Then he said, "Domingo, how did you know that Rabbi Berkowitz was still here? Do you remember all two hundred workers coming and leaving every day?"

"No, I don't remember all of them," answered Domingo. "But I remember Rabbi Berkowitz. He is different. Every day when he comes in he says, 'Good morning!' to me. And before he leaves he says, 'Have a pleasant evening!' I knew that Rabbi Berkowitz came today because he wished me a good morning. I knew he had not yet left because I was still waiting for him to wish me a pleasant evening. I knew he was still inside somewhere, and I was not going to leave until I found him."

Rabbi Berkowitz's life was saved because he made sure to greet the guard every single morning and evening.

Every person feels special when someone greets him. Let us try to be the first one to say *good morning*, *hello*, or *good night* to others.

Good Neighbor Policy

Rabbi Mattisyahu Salomon is the *mashgiach* of Beth Medrash Govoha in Lakewood, New Jersey. The Salomons live on Sixth Street, next door to the Epsteins. The two families are very friendly. Their children are similar ages and the families always help each other.

The Salomon home was filled with excitement. One of the girls was engaged and the family was busy planning for the wedding. They arranged for a wedding hall, a caterer to cook and serve all the food, a photographer, and a musician.

Only one thought saddened them. The Epsteins would not be at the wedding. Rabbi Epstein had passed away just a few months before, so the Epstein children were not allowed to attend *simchos* (happy occasions) like weddings.

"How can we celebrate the wedding without our good friends?" the Salomons thought. "There must be a way we can show them we are thinking of them, even if they are not at the wedding hall." They finally thought of an idea.

The evening of the wedding, the Epstein children came home from work and found a note on the table. It read:

To our dear friends, the Epsteins:
Please do not cook supper tonight. We will miss you at the wedding, but you are part of our simchah. The caterers will come soon with a full meal from the wedding for your whole family.

Your friends, The Salomons

A short while later, the doorbell rang. In walked waiters with trays of delicious food. There was fruit, chicken, side dishes, and even dessert!

While the Epsteins were eating, the doorbell rang again. "Can we help you?" they asked the man at the door.

"Rabbi Salomon sent me to bring you these pictures of the wedding," he answered. "I photographed the *badeken* and the *chuppah*, and brought the film to a store to be developed. Now you can see what happened just an hour ago at the wedding! The Salomons wish you could be there, but they wanted you to at least see it."

The Epsteins saw that the Salomons were real friends. Even though they were busy with their own excitement and joy, they did not forget their neighbors.

At times we may be very busy. At a family wedding, bar mitzvah, or birthday party, we may think that we are too busy to think of others. But we should not think only of ourselves. We must think, *Is everyone happy? Do they have a place to sit? Did they get food?*

Everyone feels special when they know someone else is thinking of them.